BANANA SPLIT AND BODIES

STICKY SWEET COZY MYSTERIES, BOOK 5

ALLYSSA MIRRY

SUMMER PRESCOTT BOOKS PUBLISHING

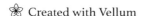 Created with Vellum

1

HIRING HUBRIS

"I'll take as much taffy as four dollars and twenty-three cents will buy."

"Mona, is everything all right?" Lydia asked.

They were standing in the center of Lydia's boardwalk shop, Doherty's Taffy and Trinkets, but Lydia had never seen anyone look so miserable buying her salt water taffy before. The young woman's eyes were red behind her glasses as if she had been crying and an air of hopelessness clung to her.

Lydia had met Mona when she had been drawn into investigating a case involving a psychic who had been murdered in their beach town. She had briefly considered Mona a suspect, but now the rightful killer was behind bars thanks to Lydia's quick-thinking. However, Lydia couldn't tell now what was upsetting the young woman.

"Your taffy is delicious, and it really helped me feel better the last time I was feeling down because of what happened to my boss. And I'm feeling pretty terrible right now too. And all the cash I have on me is four dollars and twenty-three cents."

"You know, I've been looking for somebody to try out my newest flavor and let me know if it's up to par," Lydia said kindly. "Do you think you could do that for me? It would be free because you're doing me a favor."

"All right," Mona said. "I just hope it won't be something weird like liver and onions taffy."

"Well, this might sound a little strange in taffy form, but I think it's something you'll find to be sweet."

Lydia led Mona back to her office where she kept the candy that she had been experimenting with to put her own spin on. Mona accepted a seat once they were in the room, and Lydia took out a seashell-shaped candy dish that held the colorful taffy.

Lydia was about to explain what the candy was, but Mona was too quick. She grabbed a piece of taffy and stuffed it in her mouth before Lydia had the chance to name it. Intrigued, Lydia waited to see if she would be able to identify the taste that she was going for.

"It's not liver," Mona said with a smile. "It reminds me of an ice cream sundae. But I think I also taste banana."

"You have a discerning palate," said Lydia. "That's what I was going for. This is banana split taffy."

"It's fantastic."

"Thank you for being my taste tester. Please, take as many as you'd like."

Mona took this offer to heart and grabbed two handfuls of the taffy. There was barely any left from Lydia's test batch in the dish, but Lydia didn't mind. She took one of the remaining treats for herself and waited to see if Mona would tell her what was wrong.

"Thank you for being nice to me," Mona said. "You've always been nice to me - even when you were breaking bad news to me, or we stumbled across a dead body. And I really appreciate it. I'm having a bad day."

"Why don't you tell me what's the matter," Lydia suggested. "Talking might make you feel even better than the taffy does."

"No. Because talking won't fix the problem. I moved here for a job, but with the death of my employer, I don't have it anymore. I signed a lease for a year on my apartment, thinking I'd have something to do in Ocean Point for a year. And I just talked to my landlady, and she won't let me break the lease without paying fees. And I don't really have the money for fees or rent. I barely have money for taffy."

"It sounds to me like you need a job in town," Lydia said, playing with her piece of taffy.

"I know. But I haven't had much luck with that. I went to the oddities shop, and they said I was too much of an oddball to work there. And I don't have any family that I could ask to borrow from. That's why I first got involved with someone who claimed they could talk to the dead because I really wanted to speak to my dad again. Though not to ask for money. I thought I had things under control, but it seems like I don't at all."

Lydia reached a decision inwardly and then asked, "Mona, how do you feel about taffy?"

"I love it, but I don't think it's going to solve my problems either."

Mona paused as she wondered if Lydia was implying what she thought she was. Lydia nodded.

"How would you like to work here? I've been thinking that I could use another hand as summer business starts to pick up, and I need to spend some time away from the shop trying to sell my family house."

"I'd absolutely love to work here," Mona said. "And

I'd promise just to talk about yummy taffy and not ghosts or ghouls."

"Come on," Lydia said, standing up. "I'll introduce you to the rest of the team."

She led Mona out of the office, though Mona did stop to return half of the banana split taffy that she had taken back to the candy dish. They walked back to the main section of the shop where two of her employees, Jeff and Kelsey, were joking with one another as they tidied the candy display.

"Mona, this is Kelsey and Jeff. They were the first employees I hired, and they've done nothing but make me proud. And I think you will make a great addition to the shop."

"Does she know that it's difficult to refuse eating the candy if she's surrounded by sweet salt water taffy all day?" asked Jeff.

"And does she know that working here means she'll occasionally have to help find clues?" asked Kelsey.

"I'm fine with both of those things," said Mona. "Excited, even."

"Then, welcome aboard!" Kelsey said cheerfully.

Lydia smiled. She asked Mona when she wanted to start, and Mona answered that she could immediately. Lydia thought that this would be a great afternoon to teach everyone that was working how to make her newest creation. The banana split taffy was made by combining different flavors of taffy and twisting them together. She wanted to blend vanilla ice cream with hot fudge, banana, and a cherry. All the parts were made separately and then joined together. It would be a great flavor to show Mona all the steps of the candy making from heating the ingredients to using the taffy pulling machine.

Kelsey and Jeff assured Mona that once she knew what she was doing that the candy making was easy and fun. Lydia couldn't be prouder of the way they welcomed the new girl into the fold.

She was so happy with the staff that she had assembled. Kelsey was actually someone that Lydia had babysat when she was younger. She was in high school now and had grown up into someone loyal and hardworking with a love for the theater. Jeff was strong and diligent. He was a surfer and had actually saved Lydia from drowning before when she had to swim to escape from a killer's grasp. They had both stood by her through some difficult times and were always eager to help her figure out problems – shop related or more murderous.

She also had two employees who were not working that afternoon. Annette was an older woman who crocheted creations for the shop, and Quinn was quiet but kind. Lydia thought that Mona would fit in well. After dealing with her through the course of an investigation, she knew that her heart was in the right place. All in all, Lydia thought that she couldn't ask for a more perfect team.

She was about to begin demonstrating the new flavor when the shop door opened. She turned, ready to greet a customer or possibly the handsome lifeguard that had recently started bringing her coffee.

However, she did not expect to see the person who stood in the doorway. It was the woman who ran the ice cream shop on the boardwalk and who had decided that she and Lydia should be mortal enemies because they both sold sweets. She was shooting daggers at Lydia with her eyes as she walked inside.

"I bet you're pretty happy with yourself," Amber Allen said.

Lydia didn't know what she had done, but she could see the hatred on the other woman's face.

2

AMBER'S ANGER

Lydia felt tempted to duck behind the candy counter and hide, but she thought this would send the wrong impression to her new employee. Instead, she took a few steps closer to Amber and tried to give her a friendly greeting.

"Good afternoon, Amber. How's business?"

"Business is not good, and neither is this afternoon," Amber said.

Lydia had always felt a little intimidated by the other

woman because of her gorgeous looks and her blatant dislike of her just because she owned a taffy shop. However, today, the glares that Amber was giving her brought the intimidation to a new level. She had always tried to be civil with Amber despite the ice cream shop owner's cattiness.

"I'm sorry to hear that," Lydia said.

"Are you?" Amber asked accusingly. "Because you're the one responsible for it. I had to open several hours late today because one of my machines was left on all night dispensing swirl ice cream. We had to clean up the mess and get rid of the smell before we could have any customers."

Lydia was confused. She knew that Amber thought the worst of her, but she couldn't seriously think that she would resort to sabotage, could she? How could she blame Lydia for this fiasco? It sounded to her more like a machine malfunction than the taffy shop's interference.

"That sounds like an awful morning, but I don't see how I'm responsible for it."

"It's your fault because you tricked me into hiring her," Amber said with a stomp of her foot. "You wanted me to hire Kara because you knew something like this would happen."

Lydia realized what she was referring to and tried not to laugh. She did feel bad that Cones and Cola had a delayed opening that day, but the reason was a little bit funny. When Lydia had started adding to her staff, she had been slightly paranoid about hiring a psychopath because of a murder that had just happened. Amber had taken advantage of this and had stolen applicants from the taffy shop. Though Lydia had decided not to hire Kara because she realized she did not have a great work ethic, she mentioned to Amber that she was considering making her an offer of employment. Amber immediately poached Kara and had her join her staff instead.

"I'm sorry," Lydia said. "But to be fair, you only hired Kara because you wanted to thwart me. I guess Kara brought some inadvertent karma."

"Don't pretend this wasn't your plan all along," Amber snapped. "She'd made lots of little mistakes to annoy me before, but this is what it was building toward. Wasn't it?"

"I didn't plan anything," Lydia protested.

The customers who were in her shop looking at the knickknacks and candy were starting to stare. She hoped that Amber's annoyance wouldn't dissuade them from their purchases.

She felt a little bad that Kara's incompetence had

resulted in lost time and money and apparently a stinky smell, but this wasn't really Lydia's fault. It was Amber's greed that had made her hire the girl, and it sounded like she might not have been properly trained about closing procedures.

"I knew that we were rival shops and that it would be better if there were only one place for customers to stop for a sweet treat," said Amber. "But I didn't expect you to stoop so low. I'm not going to forget this, and I'm not going to forgive."

Lydia really didn't want this to grow into a full-blown feud. Again, she tried to take the high road.

"I am sorry that you had such a bad morning and that a certain employee played a part in it. I've always thought that our two businesses could coexist because the sweets we sell are so different. Maybe I could convince some of my customers to visit your place to get a cold drink to go with their taffy."

"I don't want your charity," Amber said.

Lydia sighed. "Then, I'm not really sure what you want from me."

Amber crossed her arms but was saved from having to make a comeback by another arrival to the shop. Lydia tried not to let her annoyance show when she saw that the fight was now two-to-one. Amber's best friend, Brie Rankin, walked up to her side.

Brie worked for the local newspaper as a reporter. She wouldn't print anything that was false, but she didn't mind having a slight bias in her friend's favor. Lydia had seen this before when her taffy shop first opened.

"Why did you want to meet here?" Brie asked Amber while ignoring Lydia. "I thought you hated it here."

"I do," Amber replied. "The smell of overly sweet taffy is so strong here that I can barely stand it. But my nose is especially sensitive because of the mess I had to clean up this morning. Lydia Doherty is trying to ruin me. I thought you might want to run a story on this."

"You can't run a story because I didn't do anything," Lydia said. "Ultimately, Amber should have made sure that she had someone reliable checking her machinery at the end of the night."

"It sounds like I could write something about a feud between boardwalk owners," Brie said. "But there's a chance it might make both of your customers unhappy if they think they might get in the middle of something unpleasant."

Amber turned on her heel and headed toward the door. "Come on, Brie. We need to talk."

"If I do write a story, I'll be back to ask for your comment," Brie said before following her friend.

Amber sent one more furious glare Lydia's way before departing. As soon as she was gone, Kelsey, Jeff, and Mona were at Lydia's side.

"I'm sorry," Kelsey said. "I wanted to back you up, but I wasn't sure if interrupting her would be helpful or hurtful."

"I'm just straight up scared of that ice cream ice queen," Jeff admitted.

"It's not normally so confrontational here," Lydia assured Mona. "Normally it's rather sweet here by the shore."

Mona didn't seem scared off by Amber's appearance, but Lydia would be lying if she said she wasn't nervous. She had never seen her rival so upset before, and she wasn't sure what this meant. She hoped that there wouldn't be an ugly article about her in the paper, and she really hoped that she wasn't really a part of a feud. She just wanted to run her taffy shop in peace. Why did that have to be so difficult?

3

DINNER AND A DESIGNER DISCUSSION

Lydia tried not to think about her encounter with Amber, but she couldn't quite dispel it from her mind. She had a sinking feeling that something bad was going to happen, and she couldn't shake it. She had made sure that her taffy shop was locked up tightly that night, so no one could cause any mischief after she closed, and she tried to focus on her evening plans.

Her brother, Leo, was coming over for a late dinner so they could discuss selling the family house. The siblings had been raised by their Uncle Edgar and Aunt Edie in the house, and Lydia had returned there after their uncle had fallen ill. After his death earlier in the year, it was stated in the will that they would sell the house. When Aunt Edie returned from her world travels (that Uncle Edgar insisted she go on once he was gone), she wanted to move into a smaller house where she could make new memories instead of only focusing on the past. Lydia would also move into her own place with her dog, Sunny.

The sale of the house had been a source of tension between the siblings because while Lydia had inherited enough money and a blessing from their uncle to follow her dream and open up a taffy shop, Leo had just been left instructions on how to best sell the house.

Lydia thought that the reason why she and Aunt Edie had been left money was because they needed a little nudge towards following their dreams, and Leo had already achieved his when he became a detective for the Ocean Point police. However, it had taken a while for Leo to come to this same conclusion.

He had originally pawned off the task of selling the house to Lydia and had agonized about what he had done wrong to offend their uncle. It was only recently that Leo and Lydia had made peace and Leo seemed to remember that their uncle really did care for him.

Lydia set the takeout containers on the counter when she got home. Then, she greeted Sunny. The lazy dog had pulled herself off of one of her many dog beds around the house when she realized her favorite human had arrived home with something smelling delicious. Lydia petted the French bulldog mix and then saw the pup's pointed ears turn toward the door.

"Looks like I had excellent timing," Lydia said as Sunny wagged her tiny tail, anticipating the arrival of another Doherty that she loved.

Lydia headed to the door and opened it just as a

knock sounded. Her brother Leo grinned at the speedy greeting.

He bent down to say hello to Sunny as Lydia said, "I hope you like lo mein."

Sunny barked to inform the others that she certainly appreciated the food and Lydia chuckled as she led Leo to the kitchen table and handed him a carton.

"I love it and thanks for having me over," Leo said. "I hope I wasn't interrupting anything."

"Trina and I were thinking of having one of our girl's nights," Lydia said, referring to her best friend. "But she's sick. She thinks it's a summer cold."

"And you didn't think of inviting Daniel over?" Leo teased.

Lydia blushed when she heard the lifeguard's name but quickly recovered. "Daniel and I are just friends. Maybe it will grow into something more someday, but we're taking it slow. We both have some baggage. And be careful. If you start prying into my dating life, big brother, I'll start looking into yours."

"That's not a deterrent right now," Leo said. "There's no special lady in my life at the moment. Actually, I haven't been on a date since a disastrous blind one that the dispatcher set me up on. Still, it wasn't as bad as the ones that Aunt Edie used to send me on. Remember the time she had me go on a date with someone she said was a very sweet and kind girl, and she punched me in the face when she didn't like the dessert menu?"

Lydia laughed at the memory. "Aunt Edie tried to make it up to you by making your favorite snacks all month. I got so tired of cheese fries."

"And she still tried to set me up on blind dates!" Leo said.

It felt good to be able to reminisce and joke with one another again. Lydia could understand why Leo had been upset by the will, but she had been hurt by his cold behavior. She had missed her brother and felt like it was a time when they should have been there to comfort one another. She was glad that things seemed pretty much back to normal between them. They might drive each other crazy at times, but they also had one another's back.

"But I guess we should focus on what we need to discuss instead of my hatred toward blind dates," Leo said.

Sunny let out a small bark.

"I think that's a request for a lo mein noodle and not a comment on dating," Lydia said.

Leo pushed his half-finished food to the side and took some papers out of his pocket. He set them on the table, and Lydia leaned over to look.

"I've made a note of the important instructions that Uncle Edgar had for the best way to sell the house. I talked them over with our new realtor, and he agreed that some of the ideas might help it be bought faster."

"I can't believe Uncle Edgar made such detailed notes and that they were almost ignored."

Leo shifted uncomfortably in his chair. "Well, I wasn't in the best head space after he died. I missed him and was mad. Because he basically left me out of the will, I was afraid I had done something to offend him, and I didn't know what it was. Now, I think you're right that he was just trying to help you and Aunt Edie achieve your goals because you needed it. He knew that I would be all right. But at the time... Well, I was upset, so I decided to ignore his ideas about how to sell the house."

"I'm glad we're looking at them now," Lydia said. "I would have felt bad if we sold the house without honoring his final wishes about what to do with it as we pass it on to the next owners."

"I should have told you about his instructions earlier when I tried to push the chore of selling it off on you."

"Mistakes were made, but let's now dwell on them," Lydia said, purposefully ignoring how Leo had almost arrested her for murder around the same time. "What's the next step that we take?"

"Uncle Edgar suggested that we have a designer, Suzanne Peppercorn, work on the front porch, so it looks more inviting to potential buyers. I've emailed her, and she said she could stop by tomorrow around noon to look at it. Does that work for you? I could be here if you can't."

"No. That works fine for me. I can be here then." Sunny pushed her head against Lydia's leg to remind her of her presence, and Lydia added, "And Sunny will be here too. She'll act as a guard dog if Suzanne tries to make too drastic a change."

"I wondered if she's related to the Peppercorns who used to live in town," Leo said. "They ran a boat tour company when we were in school, but then they moved."

"I don't really remember that," Lydia admitted. She was a few years younger than her brother, but she often knew the people he spoke about from school.

"Oh, well, I had a big crush on Annie Peppercorn. So, I was somewhat devastated when the family moved. But that was a long time ago." Leo looked down as if embarrassed after admitting that. He picked at his food. "But, what's going on with you? You looked a little down when I arrived. Is it about selling the house or something else?"

"Something else, though I'm hoping it's nothing. Amber from the ice cream shop accused me of sabotaging her. I don't know if it's better to ignore her claims or fight back. I don't want to upset her too much because her best friend is a reporter."

Leo's phone began ringing, and he excused himself. "Just a minute. I need to take this."

Lydia looked down at Sunny as they heard bits and pieces of Leo's conversation. It didn't sound like good news.

"I'm sorry to eat and dash," Leo said when he walked

back into the room. "But that was my partner. I need to go to a crime scene."

"A crime scene?"

Leo paused. "I know you've gotten involved in some of my cases before even though I told you not to. But you said that you only did that because someone you cared about was involved. That's not the case this time. There's no need for you to try and do any sleuthing. Can you promise me that you'll stay out of it this time?"

Lydia didn't like being put on the spot, and she didn't like that she wasn't getting any credit for her help in putting several killers behind bars. However, he was right that she had only started investigating the crimes because they affected someone she cared about. She supposed she didn't need to put herself in harm's way for no reason.

"Fine," Lydia said. "As long as there's no pressing reason for me to get involved, then I won't."

"Thank you." Leo did indeed seem grateful with her answer.

"Did someone die?" asked Lydia. "Is this another murder case?"

"Yes. But this is my business, not yours," he said as he walked to the door and left.

Lydia frowned. Sunny moved closer to show her support and Lydia petted the dog's head. It felt strange to know that something terrible had just happened in town, but that she didn't know any details about it. Why couldn't Leo have told her anything? Now she was concerned, and her curiosity was ignited. Who was just murdered?

4

SUZANNE AND SHARING SECRETS

"And you don't have any idea what happened?" Trina asked.

"Not at all," Lydia said into her cell phone. She was trying to update her best friend on her dinner with Leo, but the fact that he was called away to a murder scene was distracting her from discussing their house selling plans.

"I didn't see anything in the paper," said Trina. Her voice sounded strange and stuffy because of her cold.

"I think it was too late for it to make it into today's paper. It was late to begin with when Leo came over. I think it was about eleven when he left."

"I hate being sick. If I was able to work at the salon, I'm sure I would have learned some details by now. I bet I would have at least learned who it was that died."

"It bothers me that I don't know," Lydia admitted. "But I'm sure Leo would have told me if it was someone that we knew that had been killed, and I know that my employees are all okay. I checked in with them before I came back home to meet the designer."

"I wish I could be there," Trina said, sounding miserable. "I'd love to see what the plans are for the house instead of sneezing on my couch."

"I'll take pictures if they do anything today," Lydia

promised. "And I'll bring you some soup and taffy later. But I should get going before Suzanne arrives."

"Okay. See if you can find out any details from Leo!"

Lydia agreed and said goodbye to her friend. She sat on her front porch with a cup of coffee and looked around. She thought that it looked homey, but it was possible that more could be done to make it eye-catching.

Sunny found a spot of sunshine to lie in and was snoozing but woke up when she heard someone approaching. Lydia was surprised to see her brother arrive.

"I didn't think you'd be here," Lydia said. "I told you I could meet the designer and I figured you'd have to work on your new case."

"I'm not going to tell you anything about the case," Leo said first thing as way of a greeting.

Lydia crossed her arms. "I wasn't asking you to. I was just surprised to see you."

He eyed her, but then seemed to be appeased. He sat down on the porch next to Sunny and started rubbing the dog's belly, making her very happy.

"I wanted to show that I was really on board with selling the house now and that I could be supportive," he said. "And Detective Grey can survive without me for an hour."

Lydia bit back her tongue. She wanted to ask how difficult the case could be if it could allow for one of its lead detectives to take care of personal business in the afternoon. Did they already have a lead and thought that it would be solved soon?

She decided to tease him about something else so she wouldn't be tempted to ask about the case immediately and put him in a bad mood right before they had company. She knew it was sweet that he was taking time off to show that he wanted to make up for abandoning Uncle Edgar's instructions earlier. She might be able to find out about the murder later on.

"Are you sure that's why you're here? And that you're not here to try and find out if this designer is related to your lost love?"

"It was seventh grade, so I hardly think it was love," Leo protested. "And I don't need to be here. I could leave if you want."

Sunny protested and pawed at his hand that had stopped petting her belly.

"I don't want you to go," said Lydia. "But I do want to

remind you of a song from our childhood, and I'll personalize it. *Leo and Annie sitting in a tree, K-I-S-S-I-N-G.*"

Leo rolled his eyes as Lydia sang the silly song. Sunny was the only one who didn't let the shenanigans distract her from the arrival of a newcomer. Though she didn't roll off her back in case she could still get tummy rubs, she let out a bark to announce the new person.

"Am I interrupting something?" the woman asked.

She had blonde hair pulled back in a bright headband. Her dress had a funky design on it, but it was partially covered with a suit jacket. She was holding a binder and looked like she was holding back laughter.

Lydia started blushing and stammered to explain why she had been acting so juvenile. However, Leo soon took the focus away from her. He jumped to his feet and took a step toward the designer.

"Annie?" he asked.

She stared at him for a moment, and then recognition dawned on her face. "Leo Doherty?"

"I didn't know you moved back here, Annie," he said.

"I go by Suzanne now instead of my nickname. But I moved back here about a year and a half ago."

"I haven't seen you around," Leo said. Lydia could tell that he was trying to sound casual, but that he was disappointed that he hadn't run into her before. He must have had a really big crush on this girl when he was in school.

"I'm always traveling these days to look at places for clients and work on designs for them," Suzanne said. "And I suppose you had a difficult year. You said in your email that your uncle passed away and that's why you needed to sell the house, right?"

"That's right," said Lydia, before introducing herself. "And it's very nice to meet you."

Sunny stepped forward, and Suzanne bent down. "And who is this? Is this your dog, Leo?"

"This is Sunny, my sister's dog. I don't have any pets right now. My job keeps me pretty busy."

"I feel the same," Suzanne agreed. "Though I would love to have a pet. And what job do you have now? I think in school you wanted to be a detective."

He nodded. "And that's what I became. I go by Detective Doherty these days."

"Congratulations," Suzanne said. "I'm impressed that you knew what you wanted to do and achieved it. It took me a long while to figure out what I wanted to do, but I think I found it."

"But you were always talented in art class," said Leo. "And my uncle obviously thought that you were skilled since he told us to hire you."

"I can't believe it's been so long. I keep running into people I used to know in Ocean Point, but it's still surprising to see how people have changed. You're really a detective now?"

Leo tried to shrug it off. "I just do my best to protect and serve."

Lydia saw an opportunity to get Leo talking and decided to take it. "He's being too modest. He does a lot to keep our community safe, and he's solved many difficult cases."

Leo smiled as he saw how impressed Suzanne looked. "I suppose I have caught a few dangerous criminals and seen my fair share of action."

"And he just started on a new murder investigation," Lydia continued. "And I'm sure he'll make short work of it."

"A murder?" Suzanne asked.

"That's right," Leo said, putting on an air of bravado. "A man was killed last night on the boardwalk. He was bludgeoned to death. But I'm sure I'll catch the person responsible soon."

"I hope so," Suzanne said, biting her lip. "It's scary to think that a killer is loose in town. The victim wasn't someone we knew from school, was it?"

"His name was Norman Nunn," said Leo.

"Norman Nunn," Lydia repeated, trying to place him.

Leo must have realized what she was up to then and clenched his jaw. He glared at her. "That's right. And it's not anyone you know, is it? And his death didn't happen by your taffy shop. So, you have no reason to get involved, right?"

"I guess not," Lydia said.

"My sister has tried to insert herself in several cases," Leo explained to Suzanne.

"If by insert, you mean *solve*," Lydia mumbled.

However, she let him change the topic of conversation away from the case and back toward changes to the porch. Suzanne seemed to think that adding a few objects would make it more attractive to potential buyers. She explained that playing up a beach or nautical theme, which was usually subtler with year-round residents, would help attract someone looking for a beach house.

"I have some things that I think could help," Suzanne said. "Would you like me to bring them over?"

"That would be great," Leo said. "I'd love to see you – I mean, I'd love to see them."

Lydia smiled. She had discovered some information about Leo's case that she could tell Trina, and it looked like hiring a decorator had been a good idea.

She might be able to speed up the sale of the house, and it didn't take a detective to see that Leo was still interested in her.

5

ANOTHER ACCUSATION

After calling Trina to tell her what she had learned and making sure that Sunny was settled into a sunbathing spot inside the house, Lydia headed to her taffy shop. Suzanne had appreciated the banana split taffy samples that Lydia had given her, and Lydia wanted to make some more of the new flavor to take her mind off of things.

She didn't want to dwell on what Amber had accused her of, and she didn't want to think about the murder when she had already said that she wouldn't investigate it. She wanted to focus on making her salt water taffy and running her business.

She entered the shop, ready to check on her employees and start a new batch of taffy. Making candy often helped her relax. She was pretty certain that even if she made an overabundance of the taffy, she could sell it or donate it.

Lydia smiled at the customers in the shop and walked up to the register to talk to Kelsey.

"How has it been this morning?" she asked.

"Well, the customers who came inside have all been pleasant, and the banana split taffy has been selling well," Kelsey said neutrally.

Lydia sensed a "but" was coming. When she didn't hear it, she asked about their newest addition to the shop. "How has Mona been fitting in?"

"Oh, she's been great," Kelsey assured her.

Jeff wandered up to the counter to join them. "Did you tell her?"

"That Mona has been a great addition?" Kelsey asked a little too boisterously. "Yes. I just told her."

"All right. What's going on?" Lydia asked, addressing her employees firmly. She knew something was bothering them, but they seemed hesitant to tell her. It might not be related to Mona, but there was something wrong.

Kelsey frowned and looked down.

"Like a band-aid," Jeff said. "It's better if we just rip it off and tell her. After all, we don't want her to be caught by surprise when..."

The shop door opened, and Jeff and Kelsey both jumped. However, when they all saw that it was a regular customer who bought taffy for the kids she babysat, the workers relaxed.

"Who are we afraid of?" Lydia asked.

"The ice cream lady," Jeff blurted out. "She's been coming around every hour looking for you."

"We told her that you weren't in," Kelsey said. "But she keeps coming back, and she won't tell us exactly what she wants to talk to you about."

"But we figured it wasn't good news," said Jeff.

"I think you're right," Lydia said. "If she keeps leaving her ice cream shop to come back here, then it must be serious."

"She looked seriously angry," said Jeff.

"After how she was yesterday, we tried to get her to calmly leave," Kelsey said. "But she does keep coming back and asking for you."

Lydia sighed. "I am glad that you told me, but I think I'm going to jump every time the door opens now."

Jeff tried to put on a chipper voice as he said, "Well, you won't have to be jumpy for long. It looks like Amber is charging this way."

Lydia turned and saw that Jeff was right. Amber Allen was headed for their door, and she looked like she was on the warpath. Lydia didn't want her employees to be forced in the middle of this again and walked over to meet her.

"Hello, Amber," Lydia said as the door opened. "I heard that you wanted to talk to me."

"So, you finally stopped hiding?" Amber said.

"I wasn't hiding. I was dealing with something outside of the business."

"If I were you, I would be afraid of showing my face around here. And it's not just because of your awful hairdos. People are going to catch on to who you really are."

"Do you want to go into my office and talk?" Lydia suggested. She didn't really want to be alone with an angry Amber, but she didn't want to frighten her customers.

"No," Amber said. "I want everyone to know what you did."

Lydia balled her hands into fists but tried to remain calm as she spoke. "I'm sorry that you've been upset with Kara's work, but this really isn't my fault. You hired her because you were trying to spite me, and you were the one who hired and supervised her. I am sorry that you lost ice cream and had to clean it all, but I'm really not responsible."

"You think this is about ice cream?" Amber demanded.

"Well, I did," Lydia said. "What are you talking about?"

"I'm talking about the lengths you would go to destroy my business. How low you would stoop."

"I didn't touch your ice cream machines," Lydia protested.

"I'm not talking about ice cold ice cream, I'm talking about cold-blooded murder!" said Amber, not bothering to keep her voice quiet.

Lydia took a step back. She was confused and disturbed by this outburst. "Murder?"

"Don't pretend that you don't know. You killed someone outside of my shop so it would be shut down."

"Amber, I didn't kill anyone. And I really don't know what you're talking about."

"A likely story," Amber scoffed. "Your brother is a detective, and you've been involved in cases before. There's no way that you wouldn't know about this."

Lydia found another reason to be annoyed that Leo hadn't wanted to share any details with her. Now, Amber thought that this was proof of her involvement. She thought that Lydia's denial was part of an act.

"I did know that a man named Norman Nunn was killed yesterday, but I had no idea it was near your shop. My brother didn't want me getting involved with his case."

"But you wouldn't even need to find out the details from him," Amber said. "Because you were the one who did this. After I closed my shop early, because of the other mess you caused, you went looking for a victim so my shop would be turned into a crime scene. You left his body right outside my shop. You're a murderer. And don't think I'm going to keep my mouth shut about this."

"I didn't even know the man," Lydia said.

"Which makes it even worse. You killed someone only to hurt me. But I'm not going to let this break me. I'm going to let everyone know what you're up to. And Brie will spread the word too. You won't be able to get away with this."

Frustration coursed through Lydia. It appeared as if nothing she said could subdue the other woman. She seemed bent on accusing Lydia no matter the facts.

"I think you should leave," Lydia said, knowing nothing else would be accomplished by their furthered conversation.

"I can't wait until I see you rotting behind bars," Amber said. "And I'm sure once I tell everyone in town, they'll feel the same. I've lived here my entire life. I didn't run away and then come crawling back."

Lydia walked over to the door and held it open.

Amber showed as much hatred as she could muster as she stormed out of the shop.

"Well, I'm glad Mona wasn't here," Lydia said, trying to joke to break the tension with her employees. "Or she wouldn't believe me that it can be calm here."

6

NO COMMENT

Lydia tried to focus on the day-to-day business of the shop, but it was difficult to focus after Amber's visit. This accusation had been even worse than the last one. Amber seemed to think that Lydia was so dead set against her that she would resort to sabotage and murder. It wasn't flattering to think that a fellow shop owner on the boardwalk could believe that of her.

Kelsey and Jeff seemed a little more at ease now that it looked like Amber wasn't going to barge in. However, they were also being protective of their boss. They kept questioning whether she was doing all right. If Lydia had been able to push her thoughts of Amber's accusations and how she planned to tell the town out of her mind, her employees reminded her when they constantly checked up on her.

They were also asking her questions about the murder, and again Lydia had to explain that she knew nothing about it. All she knew was the victim's name, that he had been bludgeoned, and that Amber considered Lydia to be the prime suspect in the case.

At least, Leo didn't seem to be taking that accusation seriously. It might be because he believed in his sister and knew that she would never be involved in a murder, or he might have been the one providing her alibi. She didn't know what time the murder occurred, but it was possible that Leo had been over at her house at the time.

"Are you sure you're all right?" Kelsey asked.

"Yes," Lydia said patiently because she knew that the

question was being repeated because her employee cared about her.

"I'd be super bummed if anyone accused me of murdering someone," Jeff said. "Especially at work and in front of people."

"I think I need to get some air," Lydia said, not wanting to revisit the embarrassing scene that had occurred before. "I'm going to take a walk."

"Whatever you need," Kelsey said. "We can take care of the shop."

Lydia thanked them and hurried out onto the board-walk. It was a beautiful and sunny day that seemed at odds with the horror that she was facing. Someone had been killed nearby, and Amber was starting rumors that she was behind it. She was afraid that Brie would start printing articles that would be technically true when it said that people in town were considering Lydia a suspect.

Her brother seemed unwilling to tell her anything about the case, so she couldn't be sure how it was progressing. She didn't know if the real killer would be caught right away and things would go back to normal or if she would have to face people looking at her like a killer forever.

To top it all off, her best friend was sick, and she couldn't spend the night commiserating with her over taffy and wine. She barely wanted to tell Trina what had happened because she didn't want to upset her when she was stuck at home sneezing.

"Lydia!"

She heard her name and turned ready to face whatever new hardship was coming her way. However, when she saw who was calling her, her frown quickly turned into a smile. Daniel was waving and walking toward her.

Her friendship with the quiet lifeguard had grown after he saved her life, and when they did some searching for clues together. Because he was a widower and Lydia was dealing with her own trust issues after how things ended with her fiancé, they were taking things slowly. They said that they were just friends, but they had gone to see a symphony together, and they had been spending time with one another, though it was often on the boardwalk.

"I can't tell you how happy I am to see you," Lydia said. "It's been a hard day, and it's barely half over."

"I heard that someone was killed near Cones and Cola," he said. "Many of the tourists on the beach were concerned about the area being designated as a crime scene."

"Which is why Amber is accusing me of the murder," Lydia recapped. "She thinks that I did it to hurt her shop. And I suppose she is losing business by having to be closed on a busy summer day, and it might hurt Cones and Cola's reputation if it is thought of as a crime scene."

"But why would she blame you?" Daniel asked, looking confused.

Lydia told him that she was about to go on a walk and asked if he would like to join her. He agreed, and they began walking in the opposite direction of the ice cream shop as Lydia explained what had happened.

"I can understand her being upset," Daniel said. "But it doesn't make any sense to blame you."

"I know. And yet it seems like my business is going to be just as affected as hers is. Her place is the crime scene, but she wants my taffy shop to be known as where the killer is hiding out."

Daniel frowned. "She was always very nice to me."

Lydia knew that this was because Daniel was extremely handsome, and Amber had been one of the women hoping to snag him. However, instead of voicing this, she just shrugged.

"You don't think there's any chance that Amber could be behind the murder?" Daniel asked. "Maybe she's blaming you as some sort of smokescreen."

"I don't know. If she did have a problem with Norman Nunn and wanted to get rid of him, then it could just be a perk to try and blame me. However, since he was found right by her business, Leo and Detective Grey must have talked to her. If they found a connection between her and the victim, then I think she would be stuck answering questions at the police station today instead of harassing me at my shop."

"Maybe there was no connection," Daniel suggested. "Maybe she killed a random person to try and frame you."

"I don't think there's been any evidence to link me to the crime so it would be a sloppy frame," Lydia said. "And I don't think it makes sense for Amber to kill someone just to hurt my business. It's basically the same thing that she is claiming I did. And I don't think that is a good motive."

"So, who do you think could be a suspect? What is your next step in the investigation?"

"I'm not involved in this investigation," Lydia said.

"Oh," Daniel said. "I guess I just assumed that you were helping with all murder cases now."

"I have to admit that the fact that it happened on the boardwalk and how Amber is trying to smear my name does make me tempted to get involved. But I promised Leo that I wouldn't. I'd need a really good reason to break that promise when we're finally starting to get along again."

"Fair enough."

They continued walking, and Lydia thought about how at ease she was beginning to feel with Daniel. He hadn't questioned her decision, but had been supportive and hadn't even considered the possibility that Amber's rumor had any merit.

However, her peaceful feeling was short-lived. She saw Brie on the boardwalk and groaned. She considered leaping over the railing and hiding in the dunes, but thought there was a good chance that Brie had already seen her and then she would be sandy for no reason.

"Here comes bad news," Lydia muttered.

Brie walked directly up to them. "Good afternoon, Lydia. I need to talk to you."

"I'm afraid I have no comment for the newspaper," Lydia responded.

"Well, I have a comment," Daniel said. "I would like to dispel any rumors that Lydia could be a murderer. That goes against everything in her character. She's an upstanding person, and I don't want to see her maligned in your paper."

Brie held up a hand. "I'm not here on behalf of the paper."

"If you're here on behalf of Amber, please tell her that I wasn't involved in what happened outside her shop."

"I know that," Brie said. "I know that you're not the killer."

"Is this some sort of trick?" asked Daniel.

Brie shook her head. "The truth is that I knew the victim. And I have concerns about his murder. But I'm not sure who I can trust. Lydia, I think I need your help."

Lydia couldn't have been more surprised by this request coming from Brie then if a seagull had landed and asked her aloud.

7

REQUEST FOR INFORMATION

"Pardon?" Lydia said. "I don't believe I heard you right. You want my help?"

"Don't make me beg," Brie said. "You're still my best friend's rival, and I don't particularly like you. But I know that you didn't kill Norman Nunn. And I think I need your help to figure out who did."

Lydia still felt dumbfounded. "But why me?"

"Because I know how you solved cases in the past. And I don't know if I can trust the police."

"Why don't you start at the beginning?" Daniel suggested.

"I really just wanted to talk to Lydia," Brie said, giving him a hard stare.

Daniel looked at Lydia instead of responding.

"I guess it would be all right," she said. She would be lying if she said that she wasn't intrigued.

He placed a hand on her arm as he said, "I'll catch up with you later to make sure you're okay. And I'll have my phone on me if you have any troubles."

She thanked him, and Daniel left. Brie waited until he was gone and then said, "I knew Norman Nunn."

"I didn't," said Lydia. "What can you tell me about him?"

Brie let out an aggravated sigh that Lydia knew wasn't directed towards her. She began walking, and Lydia followed. It seemed her walk to clear her head was continuing but in a strange new direction.

"The truth is I thought he was rather annoying," Brie admitted. "He worked at the local library as a librarian, and I ran into him before with my reporting and research. I think he developed a crush on me because he was always trying to get my attention. He started stopping by Cones and Cola because he knew I visited Amber there. I told him that I wasn't interested in him romantically, and Amber was rude to him, but he kept coming by to say hello. Then, about a week ago, he said more than hello."

"Was he harassing you and Amber?" Lydia asked, wondering if Amber might really have a motive for his murder. Maybe Brie wanted to see if there was anything she could do to protect her friend.

"No. And I don't think Amber ever paid any real attention to him. She thought of him like a fly buzzing around," Brie admitted. "And I wasn't much better. But he came into the ice cream shop recently, and he told me that he had a big news story for me. One that could make my career."

"And you think this story could be the reason why he was murdered?" asked Lydia.

"Maybe," Brie said, frowning. "I didn't take what he said seriously at the time, but now the timing looks suspicious to me. What if he did find something out and he was killed for his effort?"

"Do have any idea what the story was about?"

"Not really. He said that it involved a cover-up and high-ranking people in town. That was why I didn't put much stock in what he said before. I thought he was just trying to impress me. But if he was right, the information could have gotten him killed."

"I can understand why you were skeptical," Lydia said. "It's hard to believe that there was a big cover-up in our little beach town."

"I wanted to tell the police, but I decided it was a bad idea," Brie continued. "Since I didn't know who the higher-ups Norman was referring to were, I didn't want to inadvertently tip them off. It might even involve someone at the police station."

"It couldn't involve Leo, though. He's a very honest man."

"But if the detectives know, then the people who killed Norman might find out," said Brie. "I can't take that chance. I'll need to figure out who did this on my own. I owe it to him after I didn't believe him."

"Why do you want my help? Why trust me?" Lydia asked, suddenly suspicious.

"Because you're a nobody."

"Thanks?" Lydia said in response to the insult.

"I mean that I know you're not one of the higher-ups that Norman referred to in town. You're new and just own a candy store. You couldn't have been involved. And I need to find out who killed him if there's a chance there could be a cover-up. I owe it to him after not believing that he was on to something. But I'm not usually an investigative journalist. I normally write up reviews of the bands at Crabby Craig's or local interest stories. My crime beat is just what the police and some witnesses near the scene tell me. I don't know how to actually catch a killer. But you've done it before."

"I wasn't planning on getting involved in this," Lydia said.

"Fine," Brie said, changing direction and walking the other way. "If you don't want to help me, I'm not going to plead. And I don't want to waste any more time. I know there's something big going on in town and someone is willing to kill to keep it a secret. I'm going to figure out what it is with or without you."

Lydia jogged to catch up with her. "If someone is willing to kill to keep this quiet, I can't let you do this on your own. I'll help you."

Brie nodded. "Thank you."

"And I'll try not to tell Leo in case there's a leak at

the police station that could get back to the killer, but I'm not going to lie to him. I trust him."

"If those are your conditions, I guess I have to agree to them. But my condition is that we start right away."

"I have to make sure that my employees will be all right on their own for a longer period of time than originally planned, but then I can go," Lydia agreed. "And I think I'll grab some banana split taffy for the trip. I need a sweet pick-me-up."

"If you want," Brie said. "But I was planning on visiting the morgue first. I have a contact there who can give us some information on the victim."

"Right," Lydia said, remembering firsthand how this contact had affected the news in the past. "This is where you get your information if the police tell you no comment."

"You'll have to promise me that you won't reveal this source to your brother though."

"What if I can't?" Lydia asked.

8

THE MEDICAL EXAMINER'S OFFICE

"This is ridiculous," Lydia said.

"If you can't agree to keep a source secret, then this is the way it has to be," Brie retorted.

Lydia was feeling silly. She was seated in the waiting room outside the medical examiner's office and was wearing a blindfold. Brie had insisted that she wear it if Lydia wouldn't promise not to tell Leo who it was that talked to the press at the medical examiner's office.

Lydia didn't want to betray her brother, and she felt like he really should know if she came across the information, but the longer she sat there with the blindfold on, the more she began to reconsider this stance.

"He's here," Brie said as Lydia heard footsteps approach.

"What's going on?" a male voice asked. "What sort of news story is this? Do people want to be blindfolded near dead bodies? Is this some sort of weird trend I should be aware of?"

"No," Lydia said quickly. "And I recognize that voice. He is the medical examiner."

She had heard him before when he interacted with Leo in her presence and recently at a crime scene. She knew the voice belonged to the medical examiner, Murray McGee.

Brie grumbled, "I guess you can take off the blindfold."

Lydia complied and saw the medical examiner's confused look firsthand.

"What's going on?" he asked. "Is that Detective Doherty's sister?"

"This town is too small sometimes," Brie muttered. Then she smiled and said, "Lydia is helping me with a story, but I wanted to protect you as my source."

"I appreciate that," he said. "And what can I help you with?"

"I need to know more about the dead body, Murray."

"I figured that might be it," he said with a knowing nod.

"Because you tell Brie things about cases for the paper regularly?" asked Lydia.

"I wouldn't say regularly," said Murray. "But I have given her some inside scoops upon occasion."

Lydia wondered if this was another man who seemed to have been charmed by Brie and wanted to impress her with a great story. Was he revealing secrets about ongoing investigations to flirt with her?

"I know it was Norman Nunn who was killed," Brie said. "My friend found the body and she said that it was bloody."

"It was," Murray agreed. "But if your friend was at the crime scene, then it already sounds like you have a story. You already have enough facts to tell the people a decent amount about the death."

"But don't you think that people in town need to know everything that I can tell them about how their beloved librarian met his demise?" asked Brie. "Norman Nunn was a purveyor of information to the good townspeople. There's a good deal of interest in how he died. The people here adored him."

Murray looked saddened. He raised his fist to his chin as he thought. "People do love their librarians."

Then, Lydia realized how Brie convinced Murray to talk to her. It wasn't because he wanted to date her. He wanted to make sure that the town had the proper news.

"I can find out more about his life," Brie said. "But I need to know more about his death."

"He was bludgeoned?" Lydia suggested.

"That's right," Murray said. "The blunt force killed him. He was hit repeatedly with an object."

"Repeatedly?" said Lydia. "That makes it sound like this murder was personal. Maybe this was a crime of passion."

"Or the killer was thorough," Brie said. "He wanted to make certain that Norman Nunn was dead."

"Do you have any idea what the object that killed him was?" asked Lydia.

"It was a long cylindrical object, but it did have some weight to it. My guess is that it was a cane."

"Something that wouldn't be suspicious to see someone with on the boardwalk," Lydia said.

"What time was he killed?" asked Brie.

"Sometime between eight and ten," Murray answered.

"Amber closed the shop around six that day because of all her troubles with Kara, but she's normally open until ten on summer nights."

"Did he have anything on him?" asked Lydia.

"I think just his wallet. That's all I can tell you now," Murray said. "But I hope that's enough to describe in the paper and will allow you to honor his memory."

"Thank you," Brie said. "It will be a great article."

She and Lydia left, and Brie drove them back to the boardwalk. They started walking toward the taffy shop, discussing what they had learned.

"Well," Lydia said. "We know a little more now than we did before."

"But what Murray said is consistent with someone killing Norman to keep him quiet. They must have followed him to the ice cream shop, and when they saw that no one was around, they hit him."

"And the murder weapon is most likely a cane," Lydia said. "I wonder if any of the people that the librarian was looking into used a cane or walking stick."

"I wish I knew what he was looking into," Brie said. "I should have listened to him more."

"You don't have any idea what it was? He didn't give any hints?"

Brie threw her hands up. "He was being somewhat secretive. He wanted to make a grand reveal when he finished all his research. And I didn't take him seriously at the time. The only thing I remember was him mentioning that Lyndon Malcolm Wallace would be impressed."

"Who's that? Is he someone involved in his investigation?"

"I don't think so. He's not anyone I know of in town, and I know almost everyone. All the important people anyway. I looked him up, but the only Lyndon Malcolm Wallace I found was an author who died a hundred years ago."

"So, it's unlikely that he was involved in the cover-up or murder," Lydia said.

Brie stomped the ground. "I should have paid more attention to him."

"If he never gave you a believable story before, then you can't blame yourself for not believing it now. And if he was killed because of whatever cover-up he was investigating, then you could have been in danger too," Lydia said. "We'll make sure he receives justice by catching his killer."

"You know," Brie said thoughtfully. "You're not as annoying as Amber had me think."

"Thanks," Lydia said.

"Let's meet again tomorrow to work on this case,"

said Brie. "I'll see if I can remember anything else that Norman told me."

"I'll do what I can to figure out what he was working on too."

"See you tomorrow," Brie said.

Brie walked the opposite way as Lydia headed into Doherty's Taffy and Trinkets. If Lydia had been told yesterday that she would be investigating a case with the best friend of her rival, she wouldn't have believed it. In fact, if you had told her that she would have been civil to Brie for any reason other than not to appear unfavorably in the newspaper, she wouldn't have believed it.

However, now it seemed like she had a partner-in-solving-crime and they definitely had their work cut out for them. They had to uncover what the librarian had been working on and then determine how it related to his death. Basically, they had two cases that they needed to solve, and it seemed like they didn't have much time to figure it all out. If this was because of a cover-up and the killer had already struck once to keep the secrets hidden, he might strike again.

9

SOME DIFFICULT CONVERSATIONS

"I can't believe it," Trina said. She was on her couch under a blanket with the container of soup that Lydia had just brought her in her hand.

"I know minestrone isn't the usual soup for sickness, but the last time I brought someone chicken noodle soup it seemed unlucky," said Lydia. "And I made sure that it still tastes good with a banana split salt water taffy dessert."

"That's not what I meant," Trina said. She put the soup down on the table and tried to push it away to prove a point. However, in her tired and weakened state, it looked a bit pathetic.

"Do you want a spoon?" asked Lydia. She was standing in the doorway to the room, trying to balance helping her friend with not getting a close encounter with the germs.

"No. I want to make sure that I heard you correctly: you're investigating a case with Brie Rankin? What if this is some sort of trap so she and Amber can make you look guilty and she can write about it? Think of the quotes you could be giving her."

"I don't think Brie has any ulterior motives. She just wants to get to the bottom of this and thought that teaming up was the best way to do it," Lydia said. "I trust her."

Trina pulled her blanket closer up to her chin and pouted. "Do I need to be jealous?"

"Jealous?"

"I know that you've done some sleuthing with Daniel and that your employees have volunteered to help find clues, but I thought investigating was mostly something that we did together. I thought it was something where you needed your best friend as your backup." Trina punctuated her speech with a sneeze. "You're not replacing me, are you?"

"Of course not! I'm helping Brie because she needs me on this case, but I'd still rather have you at my side. I could never replace you. You're my best friend. And to prove it, I brought you soup and taffy."

"Maybe you should make me some apple taffy," Trina joked weakly. "I could have a piece every day to keep the doctor away."

"Actually, I think you really should see a doctor. I want you feeling better," said Lydia, "because I also really want to give you a hug to show you that you're my best friend, but I don't want to get sick."

"I wouldn't wish this cold on my worst enemy," Trina said in between sneezes. "And that might just be Amber or Brie. Be careful with them."

"I will," Lydia promised.

"And don't replace me," Trina reiterated.

Lydia reassured her again that she had no intention of replacing her. She made sure that Trina was settled and then headed home. She wanted to jump into a hot shower to wash off the germs she had been in proximity to, and then she wanted to call Daniel. She had briefly told him that she was going to check on something with Brie to let him know that she was fine, but she wanted to let him know more of the details.

However, when she reached her house, she saw that her plans would be delayed. Leo was on the porch, leaning against a pillar and staring at her as she approached. She waved as she walked up.

"Hi, there," Lydia said. "What brings you here?"

"Are you investigating Norman Nunn's death?" he asked accusingly.

"You just get straight to the point, don't you?" she said with a smile that he didn't return. "What makes you ask that?"

"Well, I heard from the medical examiner that you visited and were asking about the body."

Lydia sighed. "Murray really can't keep any secrets, can he?"

"You don't deny it, do you?"

"No," Lydia said, moving closer to the porch. "I did go to see him, but I was there with Brie Rankin."

"And you are investigating?" he said with a roll of his eyes.

"I'm helping Brie with a story," Lydia said neutrally. "I could really use some good press, and I thought it would behoove me to be in her good graces."

He stared at her as if he didn't quite believe what she was saying. Lydia didn't want him to stay in "detective mode" and continue with his interrogation. She tried to change the subject.

"I should really check on Sunny. I was gone most of the day."

Though Lydia was pretty sure that her beach bum dog was asleep somewhere in the house, she always was happy to see the pup, and it provided a nice excuse. Leo also loved the dog, and he wouldn't push back against this request.

Leo stepped aside so she could open the door and go inside. He followed her, and they found Sunny deep asleep in one of her doggy beds near a half-open window where there was a nice breeze. She looked surprised but happy when she saw two people that she loved waking her up.

She stroked the dog's ears but wasn't sure how long her French bulldog mix would distract Leo with her adorable yawns. She decided to bring up a new subject.

"So, were you also on the porch to consider Suzanne Peppercorn's ideas?"

"I did like what she had to say about playing up a nautical theme at the house," Leo said. "I could see how that would attract people. I spoke to her a little more because I had an idea. I thought we might be able to put some of the ships in bottles that Uncle Edgar used to make in the front windows. She really loved that idea. And she's going to bring over an anchor that we can place on the porch. She said that her specialty is finding interesting anchor décor. And we'll add some colorful plants too."

"It sounds like she knows what she's doing," Lydia said.

"She's a professional, and she does have natural talent," Leo said with a grin.

"And she is the girl that you used to have a crush on?"

"I bet you can see why. She's great, isn't she? I can't

believe that I haven't run into her in town before, but I guess she has been traveling a lot for work."

"And we had been distracted after Uncle Edgar got sick," Lydia pointed out. "And you do have a job that keeps you busy."

"True, but Suzanne is been back in town and has been doing design work here. I would have thought that I would pick up on the name Peppercorn being used. Once I saw that Uncle Edgar recommended her, I immediately thought of Annie."

"Maybe you thought peppercorn was a snack," Lydia joked. "I wonder if that could make for a spicy taffy flavor."

"Suzanne really liked your banana split taffy."

"It sounds like you talked to her a lot," Lydia said.

Leo shrugged. "We're just catching up a little bit. She remembers me from school, and she wants to know about the changes to the town that I noticed through the years."

"Has she asked you about your new case at all?" Lydia asked, hoping she might be able to learn more about it if it was under the guise of talking about Suzanne. "I tried to make you sound impressive in front of her."

"I told her a little about it. Women do tend to like a man in uniform who catches bad guys," said Leo. "Not that there's much to tell right now. There weren't any witnesses because the ice cream shop was closed. Amber Allen just went back that night because she wanted to double check her machinery after an apparent incident the night before. And we haven't discovered a motive after searching the victim's home. But I did try to put a positive spin on it. I think Suzanne knows what a good detective I am."

"I'm sure she does. There wasn't anything suspicious near the crime scene, was there?" Lydia asked. "You didn't find the murder weapon there?"

"With a crime so close to the ocean, there's always a chance that the killer disposed of the murder weapon in the water and..." he trailed off. "You just tricked me into telling you about the case."

"I was just making conversation."

"Lydia, don't poke your nose into my investigation," he said. "I mean it this time."

He made a jabbing motion with his finger for emphasis and then left the house. Lydia looked at Sunny, who tilted her head.

"Getting involved in this case is complicated," Lydia said. "Trina doesn't like that I'm working with Brie and Leo hates that I'm looking for clues again."

Sunny nuzzled her to make her feel better.

"Thanks, Sunny. You always cheer me up," she told the dog. "And you know what? Leo inadvertently helped too. We've been wondering what Norman discovered."

Sunny let out a small noise to show she was paying attention.

"Well, Leo just said that there was nothing at Norman's house that looked suspicious. That means he couldn't have kept his research about a cover-up there. But maybe it might be at his place of employment. And what better place to do research than at the library?"

10

LIES AND THE LIBRARY

"Once you say it, it seems obvious," Brie admitted.

She and Lydia were headed to the library that Norman Nunn had worked at to see if they could discover what exactly he had been working on. It was pretty close to Lydia's house, though she hadn't been there much since she returned to town.

"I just hope that we can convince them to let us look at his things," Lydia said.

"I think your taffy might go a long way to helping us

get some information," Brie said, referring to the box of candy that Lydia was holding. "Though the fact that you made an ice cream flavored taffy did upset Amber."

"I didn't even think of that."

"Really?" Brie asked. "We were sure that you did it on purpose to taunt Amber. She can't make a taffy flavored ice cream for her shop."

"I just like to experiment with different flavors," Lydia said. "I didn't mean anything by it. I wasn't thinking of Cones and Cola."

Brie considered her. "Maybe you're not as bad as I thought."

Lydia smiled. They entered the library and walked up to the desk. A woman with glasses on a chain pursed her lips as they approached. She barely looked up from the computer she was entering information into.

"Can I help you?"

"We hope so," Brie said. "But it's not exactly about a book."

"We brought you some salt water taffy," Lydia said, placing the box on the desk. "We wanted to let you know that we really appreciate your help."

The librarian looked at the candy box with disdain. "Taffy? You might have brought the only snack to rival gum with its danger to book pages. What am I supposed to do with this?"

"Well, I thought you'd eat and enjoy it," Lydia said, slightly taken aback.

"Look," Brie said. "You can throw out the taffy if you want. But we would like to talk to you about your coworker, Norman Nunn."

"He's not here," said the librarian. "In fact, he won't be in again. He's passed away."

"We know," said Brie. "But we think he was working on something. We need to know what it was."

"I don't know what you're talking about, but this is a library. People need silence to focus on their reading and research. I'll ask you to be quiet with your questions. And if you'll excuse me, I have a lot of work to do. We're down an employee here."

She picked up the taffy box and slid it gruffly back toward Lydia. She caught the box and looked at Brie who shrugged.

"That could have gone better," Brie said. "I guess I could have flashed my press credentials, but I don't want too many people to know who we are."

"That's right. It could be dangerous," Lydia agreed.

"It's always dangerous talking to Ms. Marsh before she's finished her coffee," a voice said.

A young librarian with frizzy hair was pushing a book cart toward them. She smiled at them, but there was sadness in her eyes.

"Don't mind Ms. Marsh. She's under more strain than usual. I guess we all are with what happened to Norman. But maybe I can help you? Did you need to find something?"

"Actually, it's about Norman that we're here," Lydia said. "We were hoping to talk to someone that worked with him."

"Did you know Norman?" the librarian asked.

Brie nodded. "We were friendly, and he was helping me with a project."

"My name is Dory. I'll do what I can to help. Norman was a great guy, and any friend of his is a friend of mine. We just should move away from Ms. Marsh."

Dory rolled her cart into the other room, and Lydia and Brie followed her.

"Were you close to Norman?" Lydia asked. "We're really sorry for your loss."

"Thank you. Is that why you brought that box of candy? That's sweet, but you shouldn't let Ms. Marsh see it again. She doesn't like food inside the building, and she has some trouble with her teeth so she hates anything that could be sticky."

"Now we find out," Brie muttered.

"But to answer your question, I think Norman and I were close. We bonded over the hardship of working for Ms. Marsh, and we had fun working together."

"Do you have any idea what Norman was working on recently?" asked Lydia. "It would have been outside of his library duties, but probably involved some research."

"I didn't know exactly what it was," Dory said. "But I know he was looking into something. He was really excited about it too. He thought the work he was doing was important."

"But you don't know what it was?" Brie prodded.

"I know that he went to the hall of records before and he had me do some tasks to help, but I didn't really understand how it related to what he was working on. I looked up blueprints for the community center for him. He also asked me about Dune Investments, but I hadn't heard of them, and he told me not to worry. He would handle it."

"Dory, we can tell that you cared about Norman," Lydia began.

"He was truly amazing. He was so smart, and he could make you laugh. I loved coming to work to see him," Dory said. "And I really liked doing research with him, even if I didn't understand the full picture. He made you feel important. He really was a great guy. But I guess you knew that if you were his friend."

Brie looked away to hide her discomfort.

"We want to find out what he was working on because we think it might have something to do with his death," Lydia admitted. "We think that he might have been on to something big. We don't want to tell too many people about this, but it sounds like he trusted you."

"You think the research that he was doing got him killed?" Dory asked with a gasp. "I've been trying to wrap my head around who would want to hurt him, but I guess this makes sense. Of course, I'll do what I can to let you know what he was doing. Do you think we should tell the police?"

"We will tell the police, eventually. I know at least one person on the force who is trustworthy, but because we don't know exactly what Norman was on to, we don't want to let too many people, or organizations know yet."

"I'm sorry to say that we might be putting you in harm's way by including you," said Brie. "But we'll try to keep this quick, so you don't seem involved."

"I'm not scared," said Dory. "I want you to find out who Norman was researching so you can find his killer. Come on. I'll take you to his locker."

She led them behind an "employees only" door.

"Be careful of the lost and found box," Dory warned as they entered.

Lydia was glad that she had been notified because it was close to the door and she almost tripped on it. Several umbrellas and a variety of other odds and ends were sticking out of it. The rest of the room wasn't much tidier. It seemed that in order to keep the main area of the library tidy, this room was filled with overflowing supplies for events.

Dory headed to some small lockers against the wall.

"Ms. Marsh and I discussed how we would need to clean out his locker, but we weren't sure which family member we should send his things to. We know that none of them live in town. But I know his combination. It's his lucky numbers highest to lowest. Maybe there's something inside that could help."

She entered the combination and swung open the locker door. Unlike the rest of the room, the locker was sparse. At first, Lydia only saw a sweatshirt hanging inside. However, then Dory grabbed something from the top shelf. It was a flash drive for a computer.

"Brie, that might have all his research," Lydia said hopefully.

"Wait a second," Dory said. "You're Brie? Norman mentioned you. He was a big fan of yours."

Brie just nodded awkwardly.

"Well, I hope that helps," Dory said. "I should get back to work. I don't want to get in trouble with the boss."

"Thank you," Lydia said, taking the flash drive. "We will do our best to catch Norman's killer. Don't worry."

"I hope that tells you everything you need to know," Dory said, before leaving the room.

Lydia held the flash drive up and grinned at Brie. "I think we might have just made a break in the case."

"Let's find a computer," said Brie.

Luckily, they were at the library, and there were public computers available for use. They kept their voices down so they wouldn't annoy the head librarian, but it was hard to control their excitement. They waited for the device to load, hoping that all the answers would be spelled out for them.

However, all Lydia could do when she finally saw what the flash drive contained was to say, "What?"

Once they pulled up the lone document on the flash drive, it revealed only a series of numbers:

25-7-17

103-4-27

213-1-15

They continued on and on. The numbers filled several pages, but the two women couldn't make sense of it. Lydia scratched her head. Maybe this wasn't quite the clue that she thought it was.

11

THE CODE

"It's strange," Daniel said. "I'm not sure what it could be."

He stared at the pages that Lydia had printed out of what had been on Norman Nunn's flash drive. Lydia had been thinking about it for the past few hours after she and Brie had parted ways at the library. She couldn't quite decide if the numbers formed some sort of code or if this was gibberish meant to confuse anyone who might be spying on him. She hoped that it held some significance for the case and kept trying to come up with different scenarios.

She was still thinking about it when Daniel asked if

she would like to grab a bite to eat for lunch at a boardwalk bistro. She knew that she wouldn't be able to hide her distraction about the numbers, so she took Daniel into her confidence. He had gained her trust as well as her affection. She also rationalized that he was too new to town to have been involved in a cover-up with the high-ranking people in Ocean Point.

"I've thought of many things that the numbers could be, but dismissed them all," said Lydia.

"It's not longitude and latitude," Daniel said, staring at the pages as he took a bite of his sandwich.

"And they're not dates or combinations that could fit into the lockers at the library," Lydia said, rattling off some of the ideas she had already discounted. She set down the rest of her sandwich, knowing that she had lost her appetite. "There's nothing else on the flash drive that we could enter the numbers into.

They're not street addresses in town or banking numbers."

"But this does mean that whatever Norman discovered is important," Daniel said. "He must not have known that it could result in his murder, but he knew it was important enough to encode."

"I just wish I knew how to decode it," Lydia said with a sigh. "The longer I take to figure it out, the longer Norman's killer is free on the streets. It also means that Brie and I could be in danger if the killer figures out that we're investigating this. And I guess we've put Dory the librarian and you in danger too."

"I can take care of myself," Daniel assured her.

She nodded, accepting this as true. She only knew a little of his Coastguard background before his wife fell ill and before he eventually moved to Ocean Point. However, she had seen him in action as a lifeguard and knew that he could be fearless when it came to saving people.

"Taking a long time to solve this also means that I have to keep Leo in the dark for longer. He's not going to be happy with me about that, and we finally started acting like we used to."

"He's not blaming you for what you inherited from your uncle anymore?" asked Daniel.

"He seems to have calmed down," said Lydia. "He's accepted that Uncle Edgar had a plan and he was helping his family in the best way he knew how. He knows that Uncle Edgar loved him."

"That's progress."

"I wish I were making progress with this code," Lydia

said, tapping the table. "It can't be license plates. I don't think."

Daniel finished his lunch as Lydia continued to consider the code. After he wiped his mouth with his napkin, signifying that he was done, he leaned forward across the table.

"There's something else strange besides the numbers," he said quietly. "I think a lot of the other diners are staring at us. At least the locals are."

Lydia sighed. "That's probably because Amber has been telling everyone who will listen that I'm a murderer who killed someone to hurt her business. I thought Brie might have stopped her, but it doesn't look like it held her back."

"Maybe there's another reason," he said, trying to sound comforting.

However, the only other reasons that Lydia could think of weren't any better. She considered that people might be staring at her because they didn't understand how the handsome new man in town was eating lunch with her, the candy lady whose hair was always pulled into a messy bun and who was often covered with patches of sugar. It might also be that someone who was staring at her was involved in whatever Norman had uncovered and was determining whether Lydia needed to be disposed of too.

"Do you want to go for a walk?" Lydia asked, suddenly not wanting to remain in the bistro amid the stares.

Daniel agreed right away. They left a tip on the table and then headed outside. They decided to walk on the beach instead of the boardwalk and dipped their toes in the water as they strolled down the shoreline. The water was still cool, but it was beginning to warm for the summer. It felt delightful on Lydia's feet as she walked along. If she wasn't concerned about a killer on the loose, it would be very relaxing.

"I don't know what I'm missing," Lydia said, finally. "I know that there must be a way to crack this number code, but I don't see how right now."

"Believe me I wish I had a book of answers for solving this too," Daniel said. "But I'm sure we'll figure it out eventually."

Lydia paused, considering what he said. It had started the gears in her head turning, and she realized a possibility for the code. However, she was so focused on her thoughts that she missed how a wave became larger as it moved toward her. Instead of lapping against her ankles, it splashed the pedal pushers she was wearing. However, she was suddenly so excited that she didn't care about her wet clothes.

"Daniel, you're a genius!" she cried.

"How so?" he asked with a smile.

"A book of answers! He was a librarian. It would make sense if his code had something to do with a book."

"I don't think it's the Dewy Decimal system or ISBN numbers."

"Maybe a book is used to decode the message," Lydia said. "The first number could be the page you turn to, the second could the paragraph, and the third is the word. Maybe this will spell out a message from Norman."

"I think you could really be on to something," Daniel said. "And I don't mean to rain on your parade, especially since you were already splashed – but there are hundreds of books at the library and millions in the world. How will you know which book he used?

If you don't use the right one, you won't get the right answer."

Lydia frowned. She knew he was right and she had already seen the inside of Norman's locker at work. It didn't contain any books. She might be able to ask Leo which books were found at Norman's house, but she bet her detective brother wouldn't want to answer her.

Before she could formulate a plan about how to best find the book that Norman might have used, something else happened to increase her frown.

Amber stormed right toward her from the boardwalk. She looked angrier than she had ever seen her before – and considering how they met the last couple times, that was saying something.

12

POINTING FINGERS

"You just have to hurt me more and more, don't you?" Amber said accusingly.

"What did I do now?" asked Lydia.

She felt like she had been showing restraint by not doing something similar to what Amber had threatened to do. Amber said that she was going to tell everyone in town that Lydia was a conniving killer. Lydia could have used actual facts to say bad things about Amber around town, but refrained.

"You're trying to steal Brie," said Amber.

"What?"

"I know that you've been going around town with her. She didn't want to tell me why she couldn't meet up with me, but I found out. And it was because of you. It's not bad enough that you sabotage my business and turn it into a crime scene? Now you need to steal my best friend too?"

Lydia tried to think of the proper response. If Brie hadn't told Amber why they were going around town, it must be because Brie didn't want the person who came after Norman to have an excuse to come after Amber. Lydia didn't want to destroy the steps Brie had taken to protect her friend, but she was also tired of being yelled at for crimes she had not committed.

"I'm not stealing Brie," Lydia assured her calmly.

"We're just working on a project together. Once it's completed, everything will go back to normal."

"I don't like the idea of her hanging out with a killer."

"I'm not a killer," Lydia protested. "I have an alibi for the murder. Right after work, I picked up takeout which I have documentation for, and then a detective was over at my house with me. I'm not to blame for this."

Amber seemed to digest what she had been told. Finally, she said, "I guess I don't know for certain that you killed that man. But if you hurt Brie, I will hurt you."

"I don't think now is the time for threats," Daniel said.

Amber finally registered that Daniel was there as well as Lydia. She tried to recover, and she fluffed her hair.

"I didn't notice you," she said, trying to sound light-hearted. "Which is strange because you're so tall, dark, and handsome. Did you just appear out of nowhere?"

"Amber, I know that you've been having a stressful time lately," he began.

"Oh, you have no idea," Amber said. "I came across a dead body near my sweet little ice cream shop, that you should stop by more often once it finally opens up again. And Lydia has been making things difficult with—"

Daniel cut her off and gently asked, "Don't you think that you should go home and recover from the shock?"

"That might not be a bad idea," she agreed.

Amber shot Lydia another dirty look but didn't say anything else. She started back toward the boardwalk.

"Thank you," Lydia said. "She doesn't listen to me at all."

"I didn't like hearing what she was saying to you."

"And I'm afraid I'm not going to make it any easier. I need to talk to Brie again. I remembered something she said, and it might lead us to the book that Norman Nunn used to write his message."

"What's that?"

"I'm not familiar with the author, but Brie mentioned that Norman said that Lyndon Malcolm Wallace would be impressed by what he was working on. We thought this might have been someone involved in the cover-up operation, but Norman might have really been making a reference to the writer. Maybe that's the book that Norman used to form the coded message."

Daniel wished her luck with her search and told her to let him know if she ran into any problems, but he needed to return to the lifeguard stand to work. Lydia called Brie and only briefly mentioned her run-in with Amber. She wanted to focus on the discovery that she had made.

Brie thought she was on to something with Lyndon Malcolm Wallace. However, she didn't know where they could find a copy of the relatively unknown author's book. Lydia suggested that they try the library.

Ms. Marsh had not seemed especially pleased to see them back at her checkout desk. However, she was more amenable to helping them find a book than answering their questions.

"We're looking for a book by Lyndon Malcolm Wallace," Lydia said. "Can you help us find it?"

Ms. Marsh typed into her computer. "We have one book by Lyndon Malcolm Wallace entitled *Catching the Corrupt and Criminal*. Let me see where it is located."

"Isn't that it there?" Lydia asked, noticing the title in a pile of books that were stacked on a shelf marked "returns."

"So it is," Ms. Marsh said.

She grabbed the book and asked for a library card.

Lydia had let her library card lapse when she had moved away for a period of time, so Brie took out hers. She ended up having to pay some fees in late fines, and she was grumbling about how Norman had always made her fees disappear as she and Lydia headed to an empty table that would provide them with some privacy.

It took a while to flip through the book and find all the correct words, but a message was starting to form. It would have been easier to read if Norman Nunn had included punctuation in his code, but his meaning was clear.

Norman addressed his message to his "beloved reporter" and told her how he hoped this story would help her career and that coding it would keep it secret. He said he hoped it wouldn't be too difficult for her to read when he handed it off to her, but that this was a crime that went up to the mayor's office.

"Am I reading this right?" Brie asked when she finished looking over the message.

"I think so," Lydia agreed. "Norman was accusing the mayor of stealing the funds raised for the community center and hiding it in a fake company called Dune Investments."

"This is a big story that could help my career," Brie admitted.

"But it's also a story that got Norman killed," said Lydia. "We'll need to be careful when we approach the mayor."

13

THE MAYOR'S OFFICE

"As I've told you, I'm not sure when the mayor will be back."

"And we've told you that we would wait," said Brie.

Lydia and Brie were situated in the lobby of the mayor's office, much to the chagrin of the mayor's assistant, Gary Sand. He kept trying to usher them out of the building, but the two women had taken seats and had no plans of rising until they had spoken to the man in charge.

"But it could be hours," Gary said, checking his fancy wristwatch.

"Good thing I brought some taffy for us to eat while we wait," said Lydia.

"Wouldn't you rather make an appointment and come back?" asked Gary.

"I thought one of the mayor's campaign promises was that he always had time for his constituents," said Brie. "Especially members of the press."

Gary held back a sigh of exasperation and checked his watch again.

"That's a very nice timepiece," Lydia said. "It looks expensive."

"It was a Christmas gift from the mayor," he said quickly. "And it's very useful for checking when he will be back, which could be a long time from now."

Brie and Lydia just smiled and waited. Lydia took some banana split taffy out of her purse and offered it to Brie. They both chewed on the snack as Gary tried not to pace around the room.

Lydia glanced about as she tried not to focus on Gary. The room was chic and comfortable at the same time without being overbearing. There was a slightly nautical theme, and there was even a shiny anchor on display on an end table.

"I like the décor," Lydia said. "We're looking at making my home more beachy at the moment too."

"The mayor hired some local woman to do it," Gary said, brushing off the topic. "But are you truly sure that you wouldn't want to come back when the mayor is certain to be in his office?"

Gary glanced at his watch again, and then the mayor walked into the room. Lydia realized that the assistant must have been trying to get rid of them before the mayor's arrival.

"Gary, what have you found out about this mess?" he demanded before noticing there were visitors.

Ned Neilson's face instantly transformed into a jovial smile. He was a middle-aged man who was trying to look younger. He wore a tropical shirt under a sports jacket and had several large rings on his fingers.

A slight limp was noticeable as he walked further into the room. He stretched out his hand to shake both of the women's.

"I'm sorry about that outburst," Mayor Neilson said. "It's so wonderful to see you both. Brie Rankin, it's always a pleasure."

"This is Lydia Doherty," Brie said, making the introduction. "She's a local business owner."

"Always happy to meet with them," the mayor said.

"Are you all right?" Lydia said, gesturing to his leg. "It looks like you hurt yourself."

"A slight knee injury from golfing," he said. "But I'm not going to let it get me down."

"I'm surprised you're not using a cane if you hurt your knee," Lydia said with a significant look at Brie. Perhaps the mayor had destroyed a cane he was using after using it as a murder weapon.

"No. I'm not someone who needs a cane. I just fight through the pain," he responded.

Lydia considered his answer. She couldn't tell whether this denial sprang from wanting to distance himself from a murder or from a desire to make himself appear tough and younger.

"Mr. Mayor, I have some serious questions for you," Brie said.

"And I wouldn't expect anything less from our local press," he said, inviting them into his inner office. "What are we discussing today? What have tourists done to offend the locals, and how can we coexist with them?"

Gary followed behind them, still looking peeved.

"It's actually a different topic of conversation," said Brie. "Do you know a man named Norman Nunn?"

"No. I've heard Nunn-thing," the mayor joked. "Who is he? Is he looking for mayoral support for a cause? I do like names with two N's in them."

"He's the man who was murdered the other day," Gary said. "On the boardwalk."

Mayor Nielson cleared his throat. "I hope what I just said can be kept off the record. I wouldn't joke about the dead. You know that. And I wouldn't want anything I said off the cuff to offend his friends and family."

"So, you don't know anything about his death?" Lydia asked.

"I did hear about a murder on the boardwalk, and I

am going to coordinate with the local police to make sure that we are all doing our part to keep our town safe," the mayor said. "But I'm not aware of all of the details. I've been busy with another matter."

"With the community center?" asked Lydia.

The mayor paused for a moment as if sizing them up. Then, he smiled broadly again.

"Yes. I know lots of money has been raised for the community center to make improvements to it, and I am eager to see them happen. I bet you think we're taking a bit too long, but sometimes the best things are worth waiting for."

"Have you raised enough funds to complete the project?" asked Brie.

"I know there has been a lot of fundraising," Lydia

said. "My friend won a raffle to benefit the community center, and I've been accepting donations in a jar at my taffy shop to support it."

"The leaky roof is something that we will need to fix," Mayor Neilson said. "And I don't have the books in front of me, but I think we are getting close so the repairs and improvements can begin."

"That's so good to hear," Brie said. "Because we believe that the man who was murdered noticed an impropriety with the money before he was killed. But you're saying that's not the case."

"An impropriety?" asked the mayor.

"Someone was taking the money and funneling it into a false company," said Lydia. "And there's been a cover-up to hide this from the public."

"No. We don't know anything about that," Mayor Neilson said. "And I'm afraid I'm going to have to cut this meeting short. Gary, we have another meeting, don't we?"

"Yes, sir," said Gary dutifully. "I'll show these women out. I'd schedule another meeting for you, but we really don't know anything about this matter."

He ushered them out forcefully. Lydia turned to Brie once they were outside.

"The mayor is lying," said Lydia. "I'm positive."

14

THE FULL SCOOP

"It's just about time to make like a banana and split," Kelsey joked.

Lydia was pulled out of her reverie. Her thoughts had been circling around the conversation that she and Brie had with the mayor ever since she returned to Doherty's Taffy and Trinkets. She wondered if there was more they could have done to get him to talk. He had rushed to get them to leave his office, so it was clear that he was upset by what they had brought up. It looked like Norman had been right. Lydia just wished that he had focused on providing evidence instead of encoding his message.

She looked around the shop. It was close to closing time, and the customers that had been inside the building had been dealt with. Mona was showing Jeff a card trick by the counter.

"That's right," Lydia said. "It's just about time to close."

"Hey. Come look at this magic trick," Jeff said, waving them over. "Mona is really good at this."

"Well, when you work for a psychic, you come in contact with magicians too," Mona said. "Or at least that's what happened for me."

She repeated the trick she showed to Jeff and correctly revealed the card that Lydia had picked.

"I still don't know how she does it," Jeff said, shaking his head in amazement.

"Those card tricks might help us sell some of our novelty cards," Lydia said. "We have several in the trinket section of the shop. Most of them have pictures of the Jersey Shore on the opposite side of the hearts and spades."

"I'd be happy to do some if you think that would help. I'm very grateful for this job," Mona said. "And it's already much better than my last one. No one here is trying to trick anyone. I mean, the card tricks are just for fun."

"Mona," Lydia said as a thought occurred to her. "I know that your last boss turned out not to be the most ethical person."

"She was a blackmailer," Mona said. "But I didn't know anything about that at the time. You have to believe me."

"I do," Lydia assured her. "I believe you. But I was wondering if your boss ever mentioned anything to you about Dune Investments. I think it's related to something that is blackmail worthy and she might have begun looking into it. And anything you know could help me with a case."

Mona thought about it. "She did say something. It was in passing, and I only remember it because of a moment of confusion. But she called it Sand's Dune Investments. Like it was someone's name. But, of course, it sounds like the sand dunes you'd find on the beach."

"Sand's Dune," Lydia repeated. "You know, the mayor's assistant has the last name Sand."

"He might be involved," Jeff said. "Could he be the killer?"

"Possibly," Lydia said. "But he might have been

doing illegal activities on behalf of the mayor and not on his own. He had a very nice watch on that he said was a gift from the mayor."

"What sort of watch is it?" asked Kelsey. "I know some things about watches because of my talks with costume designers for the theater shows I'm in."

"Well," Lydia said, trying to remember details other than it looked expensive. "It was black and had four circles of time on the front. And it had a logo that looked like a horse."

"Actually, I know it," Kelsey said. "The costume designer showed me all these magazines. I never would have thought that this would come in handy. But you're right. That logo and the four circles means it's very expensive. Like the cost of a car expensive. And it's new too. There used to be three circles on it until two months ago."

"Two months ago?" asked Lydia. "Are you sure?"

Kelsey nodded. "That's what magazine said. Why?"

"Because Gary Sand said that watch was a Christmas present from the mayor, but it couldn't have been if it came out that recently," Lydia said.

"What does this mean?" asked Mona.

"It means that Gary Sand wasn't just lying about the big things like not knowing anything about the money disappearing. He was also lying about the small things to cover his tracks," Lydia said, considering it. "It means that he's likely involved in what Norman uncovered."

"He's behind it?" asked Kelsey.

"Gary is most likely the thief who stole the money raised for the community center," Lydia agreed.

"Wow," Mona said. "I see what you guys mean about how exciting working on these cases can be. You just solved the mystery!"

"This also means I need to call Leo," Lydia said. "I'll warn Brie that I am going to, but it's time that Leo knew what we uncovered. It doesn't look like the cover-up extended to the police station, and regardless, I trust Leo and Detective Grey. And everything we've deduced is circumstantial right now. He'll have to find some hard evidence to get charges to stick."

"It was really mean to rob the community like that," said Jeff. "Hopefully your brother can find the money and make sure that the community center still gets it."

"I just hope that he'll be so happy that I'm telling

him about a murderer before they come after me that it makes him forget how long I took to tell him what I learned," Lydia said.

She braced herself as she took out her cell phone and made the call, keeping her fingers on the other hand crossed for good luck.

15

MOTIVES

"And that's all there is?" Trina asked on the phone.

"That's all there is," Lydia agreed on her end of the call.

Lydia was home relaxing on the couch with Sunny and some banana split taffy after a long conversation with Leo. Though he wasn't thrilled with Lydia keeping Norman's research quiet for so long, he did appreciate that she told him about the culprit without going off and setting a trap on her own. She'd had mixed results with facing killers in the past and had found herself in dangerous situations.

Leo seemed glad that he would be the one to track down the final needed clues and catch the killer in a by-the-book manner.

"So, you just told Leo what you discovered, and that was the end of it?" asked Trina. "You didn't try and trap the killer into saying something and ignite his wrath? And you weren't nearly killed?"

"You're sounding better," Lydia said instead of answering.

"I'm feeling better," Trina agreed. "My sneezing has abated, and I don't feel as weak. I bet after one more night of sleep, I should be back to my not-so-old self. We could have a girl's night. That is if you don't have plans with Brie."

"I told you that working with Brie was just because of the case," said Lydia. "You're irreplaceable as my best friend. And we didn't even go out to celebrate the solving of this case. I'm home sitting with a sleepy dog and Brie is getting some quotes for her article. She's meeting Dory for some background on Norman's research process."

"I'm glad I'm not replaced," Trina said. "And for the next case, I want to be really helpful. I'm not sitting the next one out."

"I'm not sure I want there to be a next one. But if there is, I'd love for your support."

"I could start tomorrow," said Trina. "In fact, if there are any last-minute things you need to be done for this case, I could do it. I won't sneeze or wheeze on anyone. I promise."

"I told you. I'm finished with this case. Leo is going to find the proof to link Gary Sand to Dune Investments. The theft will be obvious, and that provides the motive for Norman's murder. Leo and Detective Grey have it under control," Lydia said.

"I guess you're right. This Gary guy was keeping very busy, stealing money and keeping tabs on people who might have found out. And then murdering them."

Lydia heard a whistling sound in the background of her call.

"That's my hot water," Trina said. "I'm going to have some sleepy time tea and tomorrow I should wake up all better."

Lydia expressed that she hoped that this was the case and bid her friend good night. However, the relaxing feeling that Lydia had started to feel, knowing that the case was done had disappeared. Something that Trina had said bothered her.

Lydia got to her feet and started walking around. Sunny watched her and listened, and Lydia talked through her thoughts.

"I'm overthinking it now. I'm sure I am. But... Trina might have just raised a good point. How did Gary Sand know that Norman was on to him? Could he really have been keeping tabs on everyone who might have had a suspicion about the community center money? It is possible, but is it likely?"

Sunny rolled over to a more comfortable spot but kept watching Lydia.

"Maybe Gary Sand is guilty of the theft, but not of the murder. Maybe he did embezzle the money and worked to cover it up. But maybe this cover-up didn't include murder."

Sunny barked.

"I know," said Lydia. "If it wasn't Gary Sand, then who is the killer? I don't know the answer to that. But it's all right. I don't need the answer. Leo and Detective Grey can solve it. I told Leo that I wouldn't interfere with his cases unless I needed to, and I don't need to. Brie and I finally decided it was safe to share Norman's work with the police. They have all the clues now. They can figure it out."

Having decided this aloud, Lydia sat back down on the couch, ready to cuddle with Sunny and watch some TV. However, as soon as she sat, a terrible thought entered her mind. As soon as it did, more pieces of the puzzles began to fit together. She suddenly knew that Gary wasn't the killer.

"Norman's note," Lydia murmured. "He said that he was handing Brie the code. But he never actually did. It was in his locker. And the book…"

She suddenly knew exactly who the killer was, and this realization didn't fill her with any joy.

"I need to call Leo," she told Sunny frantically. "Brie is in trouble."

16

THE RESCUE

Lydia tried to quiet her ragged breathing. The library was within walking distance from her house, but she had run the entire way there. She had called Leo as she raced there and explained the situation. He had commanded her not to go inside alone, but she had hung up before answering him. She knew that Brie's only chance might be having another witness at the scene.

She tried the main entrance and was grateful to discover that it was unlocked. She entered quietly, trying to get her bearing on the situation before she was noticed. She thought that she might only need to distract the killer for a little while. Leo and Detective Grey were on their way. However, they had been on the other side of town looking into the embez-zlement.

Lydia heard a cry and crept toward the sound.

"You don't have to do this," Brie said.

Lydia peeked through the bookshelves and saw that Dory was wielding a knife. Brie looked terrified. Lydia knew that she needed to help her.

"You're the reason I have to do this," Dory said. "It was all your fault."

She moved the knife closer to the cowering Brie. Lydia wasn't sure what the best move was, but she knew that she had to take some sort of action. She pushed the books in front of her off the shelf, so they fell with a thundering thud. Then, she hurried out of sight.

Dory jumped and then went to investigate.

"Don't try to run," she warned Brie.

Lydia managed to evade Dory and stay out of her view. However, she positioned herself so that Brie could see her.

"Get her talking," Lydia mouthed. "Stall."

Brie looked as if she might pass out from fright, but she followed the instructions as Dory left the pile of fallen books.

"You killed Norman?" Brie asked. "But you were his friend."

"That's right," Dory said. "His friend. I should have been more than his friend. We were meant for each other. If you saw the way we were together, you would have agreed. But he was obsessed with you. And why? You were awful to him. You used him. And he still wanted to impress you. I thought he finally came to his senses when we started doing research together. But he couldn't get out from under your spell. I saw him waiting by the closed ice cream stand, hoping you would be there and it sickened me. I called him out on it, and he didn't care. Suddenly, I couldn't look at him anymore. And I just started hitting him."

"And you had a cane?" asked Brie.

Lydia was impressed with Brie's follow up question. However, Lydia was putting another plan into action as well. She grabbed a heavy book and walked as quietly as she could down the aisle.

"I took it from the lost and found," Dory said.

"People leave the strangest things here. I guess I must have had some thoughts of what I was going to do when I left the library with it. But I hoped that Norman would prove me wrong. He was supposed to love me."

"I'm sorry," Brie said.

"You should be."

"But killing me isn't going to fix things. It's only going to make it worse. You won't be able to get away with it."

"Yes, I will," said Dory. "I'm not stupid. I'm not going to kill you here. We're going to go someplace where it will look like the same people who killed Norman attacked you to cover up what they did. Thank you for telling me it was the mayor and his assistant. The question is: should we leave your body by their office or should he have murdered you on the boardwalk too?"

Lydia didn't let Dory reach an answer to the question. She raced around the corner and caught Dory by surprise. Using the book, she knocked the knife out of her hand.

Dory cried out in pain, but Lydia didn't stop. She hurried to pick up the knife first.

"Stay right there," Lydia said. "The police are coming."

"But Brie has to die," Dory said, beginning to sob. "She's really the one who killed Norman. I had to do it. Because of her. It's her fault."

Dory's sobs were soon interrupted by the arrival of the police. Leo and Detective Grey entered with their weapons drawn. Lydia dropped the knife when she saw them.

"We're all okay," she reported. "We're not hurt."

Leo slapped some cuffs on Dory who was having trouble remaining silent despite being warned of her right to do so. She kept screaming and cursing Brie's name. The two detectives worked together to escort her out of the building.

"You saved me," Brie said, walking towards Lydia.

"I just wish I had realized she was the killer earlier," Lydia replied. "Before you went to meet with her."

"How did you figure out it was her?"

"Well, Trina said something to make me doubt Gary

Sand's guilt as the murderer. And then I started thinking about the message we decoded. It was written as if Norman had given you the message like a letter. And then I realized that must have been what he intended to do if he had met you at Cones and Cola that night."

"I still don't understand."

"I think he would have given you the flash drive and he would have handed you the book so you could decipher the code," Lydia said.

"I guess that does make sense based on his message. He would have felt like a spy handing me the book and coded message. He would have thought I would be impressed."

"When I realized that they weren't found with the body, I had to figure out what happened to them. The killer must have taken them. Dory took them.

The librarian in her wouldn't let the Lyndon Malcolm Wallace book be ruined. She placed it on the return shelf at the library. And she put the flash drive in his locker, hoping someone would find it."

"She wanted the police to blame the person that Norman had uncovered as a thief," said Brie.

"Exactly."

"Well, I don't think I'm going to make a habit of investigating anymore," Brie said. "This was too close a call for me."

Lydia nodded. "Though I can't wait to see what you write up in the newspaper about this."

EPILOGUE

Lydia folded up the local newspaper gruffly and set it aside with a huff.

"Bad news?" Leo asked.

Lydia had been sitting on the front porch, reading the paper, but stood up to greet him. Sunny waddled over to say hello and to sniff the potted plant that he was carrying.

"It's not necessarily bad news," Lydia said. "But I

wasn't mentioned in Brie's article about the murder at all."

"Do you think she was respecting your privacy?" asked Leo.

"I think she didn't want Amber to see in writing that I acted heroically and saved Brie's life."

"About that," Leo said, setting down the pot and allowing Sunny to better sniff the flowers. "I'm glad that no one was hurt and I know your actions helped secure that outcome, but I really can't have my little sister rushing off after murderers. That's my job, okay?"

Lydia just nodded.

Leo chose to change the subject as he didn't think he

would get another promise of noninvolvement in future cases. "What do you think of the flowers?"

"They're pretty. And I think they will be eye-catching. Was this part of Suzanne's advice?"

"Yeah. We went to pick out some plants for the house together. She has a great eye. She's a very talented decorator," Leo said.

"I know. She even designed the mayor's office," Lydia said. "Though I don't think she'll be advertising that right now. Gary Sand might have been the thief and not the mayor, but Mayor Nielson should not have kept the stolen money a secret just because he was embarrassed by it."

"Right," Leo said. He looked off dreamily. "I had a really nice time with Suzanne at the garden center."

"And?" Lydia asked, sensing that there was more to the story that he wanted to tell her.

"And we're going out to dinner Friday night," Leo said, all smiles. "We just really seem to click. I don't want to jinx it. But I haven't felt this way about someone before. I'm really glad that Uncle Edgar decided we needed a decorator."

"Leo," Lydia said, playfully hitting his shoulder. "You're a detective. Can't you see what happened?"

"What?" he asked, sounding genuinely confused.

"All this time, we thought that Uncle Edgar didn't leave you anything in his will, but we were wrong."

"What do you mean?"

"His instructions on how to sell the house were in front of us the whole time. We were just ignoring them. He wanted you to see Suzanne again. He knew that you two would hit it off, and he hoped you might have a future together," Lydia said, happily. "That's the dream that he was helping you realize and you didn't need money for it. He was helping you find true love."

Leo looked dumbstruck for a moment and then shook his head. "No. There's no way. If he just wanted me to meet Suzanne, he would have said so."

"No. It had to be this way. You despised blind dates that Aunt Edie sent you on and you wouldn't have been open to the idea. You would have rebelled. And if you thought of this as a final request, you wouldn't have been able to focus on Suzanne as a person. You'd only think of the relationship as a duty. What he did was thoughtful and perfect," Lydia said. "And the only reason I'm pointing this out is so that you'll finally get it into that head of yours that Uncle Edgar didn't abandon you. He knew you and loved you."

Lydia didn't think it was possible for Leo's smile to get any bigger, but it did. She started grinning as well.

"Did you see Aunt Edie's latest postcard?" Lydia asked, slightly changing the subject. "It was from Paris."

"The city of love," Leo agreed. "And I think she gave some pretty good advice in mine."

"Mine too," Lydia agreed. "She said to cherish the people you care about as much as you can while you have them."

"Really?" Leo joked. "In mine, she just told me I should try a baguette and cheese!"

They both laughed, and Sunny joined in with a happy bark.

AUTHOR'S NOTE

I'd love to hear your thoughts on my books, the storylines, and anything else that you'd like to comment on—reader feedback is very important to me. My contact information, along with some other helpful links, is listed below. If you'd like to be on my list of "folks to contact" with updates, release and sales notifications, etc.... just shoot me an email and let me know. Thanks for reading!

Also...

... if you're looking for more great reads, I am proud to announce that Summer Prescott Books publishes several popular series by Cozy authors Summer Prescott, Gretchen Allen, Patti Benning, as well as Carolyn Q. Hunter, Blair Merrin, Susie Gayle and more!

CONTACT SUMMER PRESCOTT BOOKS PUBLISHING

Twitter: @summerprescott1

Blog and Book Catalog: http://summerprescottbooks.com

Email: summer.prescott.cozies@gmail.com

And...look up The Summer Prescott Fan Page and Summer Prescott Publishing Page on Facebook – let's be friends!

To download a free book, and sign up for our fun and exciting newsletter, which will give you opportunities to win prizes and swag, enter contests, and be the first to know about New Releases, click here: http://summerprescottbooks.com

Printed in Great Britain
by Amazon

85814114R00113